Which came first,
the chicken or the egg?
The mystery grows
and grows.
But it has been said that
the rooster knows,
and that is why he
crows and **crows**.

With love to my daughter, Susie, and her inspirational chickens! – B. W.
For my kids, Facundo and Olivia, and their love of nature – V. C.

Barefoot Books
294 Banbury Road
Oxford, OX2 7ED

Barefoot Books
2067 Massachusetts Ave
Cambridge, MA 02140

First published in Great Britain by Barefoot Books, Ltd
and in the United States of America by Barefoot Books, Inc in 2015
The paperback edition first published in 2015

Graphic design by Ryan Scheife, Mayfly Design, Minneapolis, USA
Reproduction by Bright Arts (HK) Ltd, Hong Kong
Printed in China on 100% acid-free paper
This book was typeset in MB Bokka, Bodoni and Chelsea Market Pro Regular
The illustrations were prepared in acrylics on paper

Hardback ISBN 978-1-78285-082-3
Paperback ISBN 978-1-78285-083-0

British Cataloguing-in-Publication Data:
a catalogue record for this book is available from the British Library

Library of Congress Cataloging-in-Publication Data
is available under LCCN 2013029605

1 3 5 7 9 8 6 4 2

Millie's Chickens

Written by Brenda Williams

Illustrated by Valeria Cis

Barefoot Books
Step inside a story

Here's Millie's **rooster**,
Happy and proud,
Greeting the world
By **crowing** out loud.

Cock-a-

doodle doo!

Here are the **hens**,
strutting around,
Free to wander
And peck at the ground.

Here is Millie,
Up at dawn,
Feeding her chickens
Pellets of **corn**.

Here is **Silkie**,
Friendly and calm,
Happily tucked
Under Millie's arm.

Here is **Rhodie**,
Heavy and round.
She lays eggs
That are big and brown.

Here is **Leggy**,
Who lays blue eggs,
Strutting around
On long, slim legs.

Here is Millie,

Looking around.

But where is Silkie?

She can't be found!

Here is Silkie,
Hiding away,
Finding a place
Where she can **lay**.

Here's Silkie's **nest**.
  She's such a good mother;
She's happy to care
  For her own eggs and others.

Here are the **chicks**,
Hatching out well,
Pecking their way
From inside the shell.

Here is the **water**
The little chicks need.
They drink it all up
To wash down their **feed**.

Here is the **hopper**,
  Filled with grit every day
To strengthen the shells
  Of the eggs the hens lay.

Here is the **sunshine.**

The warm spring weather
Helps the chicks grow
Their grown-up **feathers**.

Here is the house,
Called a **coop** or an **ark**,
Where the hens go to bed
As soon as it's dark.

Here is Millie.
She shuts the doors **tight**,
Keeping her chickens
Safe through the night.

Here is the **fox**,
Snooping around.
But all of the chickens
Sleep safe and sound.

Here is the morning.
Millie opens the pen.
The chickens **roam free**
In the garden again.

Here's Millie's **basket**.
She puts the eggs in.
With cream, brown and blue ones,
It's full to the brim.

Here are the **eggs**
For **Millie** to eat
With hot toast and butter –
A delicious treat.

About Chickens

Chickens come in many shapes and sizes. Baby chickens are called chicks, but once a chick starts to grow it is called different names. Female chicks become pullets at around eight weeks old. They become hens when they are old enough to lay eggs.

Only hens lay eggs. They lay fewer and fewer eggs as they grow older. Most hens over three years old don't lay eggs at all.

Young male chickens are called cockerels, and are then called cocks or roosters when they are fully grown. Chickens are fully grown when they are one year old.

rooster

hen

cockerel

chick

pullet

Breeds of Chicken

There are hundreds of chicken breeds. The three kinds of hens Millie keeps are very friendly and good natured. These three breeds are all excellent chickens for children to keep.

Rhode Island Red

These chickens are not always red; sometimes their plumage is so dark that it looks maroon, and sometimes it has white streaks. Their eggs are light brown. People like raising Rhode Island Reds because they are strong, sturdy birds that lay lots of eggs. The breed is the state bird of Rhode Island, USA, where it was first bred in the late 1800s.

Cream Legbar

You can identify male and female Legbars as soon as they hatch. Male chicks have a lighter plumage than females, and usually a cream spot on their heads. Cream Legbars are good egg layers. Their eggs are usually light blue but can also be olive green.

Silkie

Silkies are calm and friendly. They have special fluffy feathers that look like hair and feel very smooth. Silkie hens are not very good at laying eggs, but they are excellent mothers. They are quite happy to look after another chicken's eggs. Their own eggs are creamy white. Most chickens have four toes, but the Silkie has five.

Rhode Island Red

Cream Legbar

Silkie

Roosters

Perhaps because he likes to roost, or sit resting on a high perch, a fully grown cockerel is often called a rooster. In the same way that many birds sing, he will crow loudly first thing in the morning to mark his territory. A happy rooster will also crow at any time of day, or even at night if he's disturbed. A rooster will protect his hens; some roosters even fight off attacks by predators like dogs and foxes.

Keeping Chickens

Chickens make lovely pets. They are easy to keep and can live in gardens or backyards as well as on larger areas of land. Chickens need a safe, fox-proof coop, food twice a day and plenty of fresh water, grit and clean straw or sawdust in their coop.

Chickens can only fly very short distances so you don't need to worry about them escaping. Keeping chickens as pets can be a rewarding experience. Not only are their fresh eggs delicious to eat and very good for you, but they are social birds and can enjoy being handled, like Silkie does!

Anatomy

The red crest on the top of a chicken's head is called a comb. The red flap under a chicken's neck is called a wattle. Male chickens often have larger combs and wattles than the females.

Like all birds, chickens have a beak but no teeth. Because they can't chew their food, they have two stomachs. The first stomach is called the crop, and the second stomach is called a gizzard. The gizzard has muscular walls and helps the chicken to digest food.

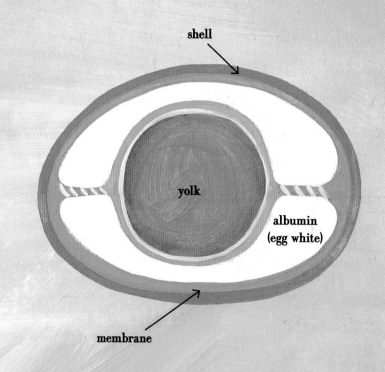

shell

yolk

albumin (egg white)

membrane

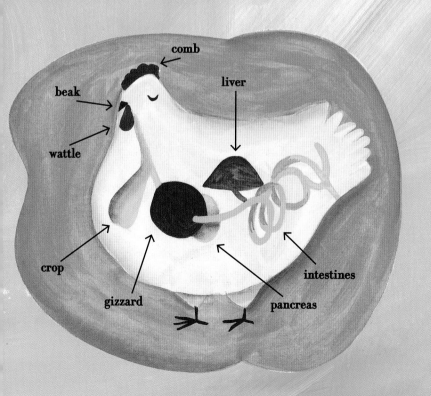

comb

liver

beak

wattle

crop

gizzard

intestines

pancreas

Parts of an Egg

Different breeds of chicken lay eggs with shells of different shades — white, brown, cream, blue and even pale green! Inside the hard shell a clear, watery liquid, called albumin, protects the yolk. It's also called the egg white because it turns bright white when cooked. The yolk, or orange-yellow part of the egg, floats in the middle of the egg white.

Feeding

Chickens eat seeds, grains and insects. Young chicks need food that is high in protein. Grit helps chickens to digest their food. It also helps strengthen the shells of the eggs they lay. Free-range hens eat grasses and insects in addition to their grain, and their eggs are healthier for us to eat because of this balanced diet.

Breeding Chickens

A hen will start to lay eggs when she is about six months old. If hens are kept with a rooster then their eggs may be fertilized. Only fertilized eggs will grow into chicks.

For chicks to hatch, fertilized eggs need to be kept in a warm place: either under a broody hen, like Silkie, or in an incubator that uses special lights to give off heat. It takes twenty-one days for fertilized eggs to hatch into chicks.

Collecting Eggs

Eggs need to be collected every day. It's important not to keep them for too long before you eat them. Old eggs go bad, and eating them can make you sick. Rotten eggs are very smelly!

To check if an egg is fresh, put it in a bowl of water. Fresh eggs will sink, and older eggs will float, because air seeps into the shells as they age. If an egg floats, don't eat it!

Eating Eggs

Eggs taste best if you eat them on the day that they are laid. Free-range hens that are raised outdoors with lots of space lay eggs that are tastier and better for you than eggs from hens that are kept inside.

Eggs are delicious and can be eaten in lots of different ways. They are also rich in protein and vitamin D.

Cooking Eggs

There are lots of ways to cook eggs. These are some of them. We also use eggs in cakes, muffins, pancakes and other dishes.

Poached

Eggs are usually poached in water. Bring a pan of water to a gentle boil, then turn it down to a simmer. Stir a little whirlpool into the middle of the liquid then crack an egg into a cup and carefully pour the egg from the cup into the whirlpool. When the white of the egg becomes firm, the egg is ready to eat.

Fried

Fried eggs are cooked in a pan with butter, lard, oil or bacon fat. Heat up a greased frying pan to medium-high heat and crack an egg straight into the pan. When the white part is solid, the egg is done!

Hard-Boiled

Boiled eggs are cooked inside their shells. First, bring a pan of water to a rolling boil. Then carefully lower in the eggs with a spoon, making sure that the shell doesn't crack. Boil for about ten minutes to cook the egg completely, or take it out after three or four minutes if you want your egg to be soft-boiled.

Scrambled

To scramble eggs, mix the yolks and whites of two or three eggs together in a bowl with a little milk, salt and pepper. Pour the mixture into a greased frying pan or saucepan and stir it over a low heat with a wooden spoon or spatula. Scrambled eggs are especially good with bacon, herbs or cheese.